Just Like Sisters

For Matilda, Thomasin, and Beatrice
—A. McA.
To my beloved sister Zebrina
—S. F.

Atheneum Books for Young Readers
An imprint of Simon & Schuster Children's Publishing Division
1230 Avenue of the Americas, New York, New York 10020
Text copyright © 2005 by Angela McAllister
Illustrations copyright © 2005 by Sophie Fatus
First published in Great Britain in 2005 by Simon & Schuster UK Ltd.
1st U.S. edition, 2006
The text for this book is set in Bodoni Book.
Manufactured in China
2 4 6 8 10 9 7 5 3 1
Library of Congress Cataloging-in-Publication Data
McAllister, Angela.
Just like sisters / Angela McAllister ; illustrated by Sophie Fatus.— 1st ed.
p. cm.
"An Anne Schwartz Book."
Summary: When Nancy and her accident-prone pen pal Ally meet for the first time,
the unlikely duo discover that they are more like sisters than just good friends.
ISBN 1-4169-0643-6 (ISBN-13: 978-1-4169-0643-8)
[1. Pen pals—Fiction. 2. Friendship—Fiction. 3. Alligators—Fiction.] I. Fatus, Sophie, ill. II. Title.
PZ7.M11714Ju 2006
[E]—dc22
2004029180

Just Like Sisters

Angela McAllister & Sophie Fatus

An Anne Schwartz Book
Atheneum Books for Young Readers
NEW YORK LONDON TORONTO SYDNEY

Nancy's pen pal was coming to visit from Florida.

Dear Nance,
At last we're going
to meet. I'm so excited!
My plane arrives on
Saturday morning.
Love ALLYxx

Nancy read all of Ally's letters over again.
"We know each other so well, we're almost like
sisters," she said happily.

Ally's plane was right on time.

"Nance!" cried Ally. "You're exactly how I imagined."

She gave her a big hug.

"So are you," said Nancy.

"How was your flight?" asked Nancy's mom.

"Great!" said Ally. "They showed my favorite movie."

Nancy took her friend's hand and squeezed it.

"I'm so happy you're here at last," she said.

On the way back from the airport they stopped at the pizza parlor. Ally ate nine Spicy Shrimp pizzas and broke a chair. "It's okay," she said. "My mom gave me extra money for accidents."

When they got home, Nancy took Ally straight up to her bedroom.

"These are my treasures," she said. Ally loved them all.

Then Ally got out her photo album. "This is my brother, Snap.

He'll be so handsome when his braces come off," she sighed.

Nancy played her favorite songs and Ally taught her
to dance the Swamp Stomp and the Crazy Creek Creep
until they both fell down laughing.

"You're not like any of my other friends, Ally," said Nancy.

"Don't they like to dance?" asked Ally.

Later on, Dad popped his head into the doorway.

"Would you girls like to share the big bed?" he said.

"Mom and I can sleep in the bunks."

But Nancy and Ally were too excited to go to sleep.
They tried on Mom's lipstick, watched videos, and
finished two cartons of ice cream.

The next day Nancy and Ally went shopping.

They bought everything exactly the same.

"I've never worn pink before. I think it looks good on me,"

said Nancy happily.

"I bet people will think we're twins," said Ally.

Nancy took Ally to the swimming pool.

"She's my pen pal," Nancy told the girls proudly.

"All the way from Florida."

Ally headed straight for the diving board.

"Look out below!" she yelled.

Ally wanted to do everything Nancy did.

She joined in Nancy's ballet class.

"Think of yourselves as young trees

gently waving in the breeze," said Madame.

Ally thought of herself as a tree.

"You look like a log, dear," said Madame.

But at the end of the class Ally gave

a special performance.

"I'm an enchanted log!" she cried with a twirl.

"Magnificent!" gasped Madame.

That afternoon the girls went rollerskating in the park.

"Look at me," cried Ally. "I'm flying!"

And she flew straight into a bush.

Later, when Ally got her skating legs,

she gave everyone a ride.

On Ally's last day, the girls went to the beach.

They built sandcastles and played frisbee.

Then a boy in trouble called for help.

"I'll save you!" cried Ally, and she zoomed toward him
like a torpedo.

When he saw Ally, the boy suddenly remembered how to swim,

but she rescued him anyway.

That evening Nancy and Ally made friendship

bracelets for each other.

"I'll always wear this and think of you," said Nancy.

"I don't want to go home tomorrow," said Ally.

All of Ally's new friends came to see her off at the airport.

The man taking the baggage peered over his desk.

"Is your sister going too?" he asked Ally.

Nancy and Ally beamed.

"Sisters are together even when they're apart," said Nancy.

"Always and forever," said Ally.